THE

AMBITIOUS BAKER'S

BATTER

Written and illustrated by

Wendy Seese

for Brittany and Dustin

Red Wheelbarrow Press

Austin, Texas

This book may be ordered by writing to Red Wheelbarrow Press, Inc., P.O. Box 33143, Austin, Texas 78764. Please include $2.50 for shipping within the United States. Texas residents add 8.25% sales tax. Order information is also available on our website: www.rwpress.com.

Library of Congress Catalog Card Number 97-68563

ISBN 0-9659961-0-7

Printed in the United States of America

Once upon a time, there was a very ambitious doughnut maker who woke up early every morning to make doughnuts. Eventually, he grew tired of making doughnuts and wanted to make something more important. He wanted to make a world. The doughnut maker decided to learn everything he could.

He read over recipes
and history books,
drew pictures of poets,
cut clippings of crooks.
He analyzed androids,
looked over lists,
listened to sunshine
and untwisted twists.

The doughnut maker thought he was ready to begin his world. He closed up shop early and collected his toolbox, his wooden spoon, his blender and–most importantly– an enormous mixing bowl, and then . . . .

he started with ketchup
and a garden of rocks,
added toy soldiers
and an athlete's old socks.
He mashed in potatoes.
He poured
and puréed.
He extracted the noise from a circus parade.
He mooshed.
He squished,
furled and twirled,
thumped,
whumped
and whirled the world.
He whisked up hope
with a bundle of rope . . .
and as the world began to take shape,
he threw in confetti,
blue cheese dressing,
paper, ribbons and tape.

The doughnut maker rolled the concoction into a big doughball and put it in the oven overnight at 110 degrees—only to wake up and discover that the world he'd been working on most of the night still, in the morning, wasn't quite right.

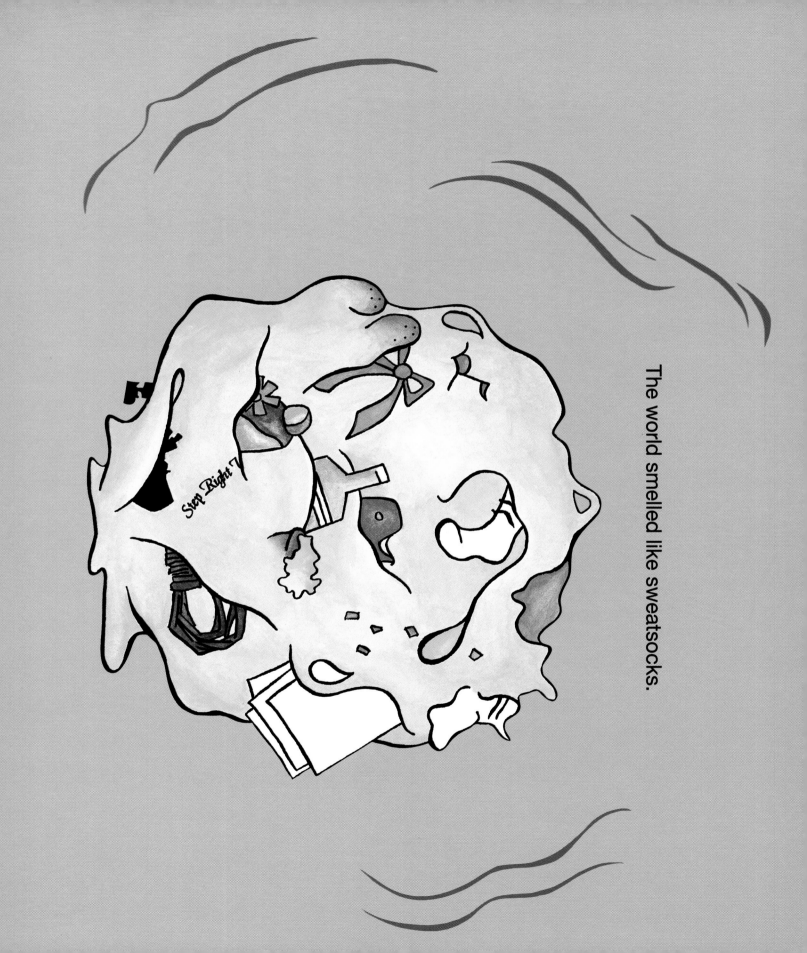

The world smelled like sweatsocks.

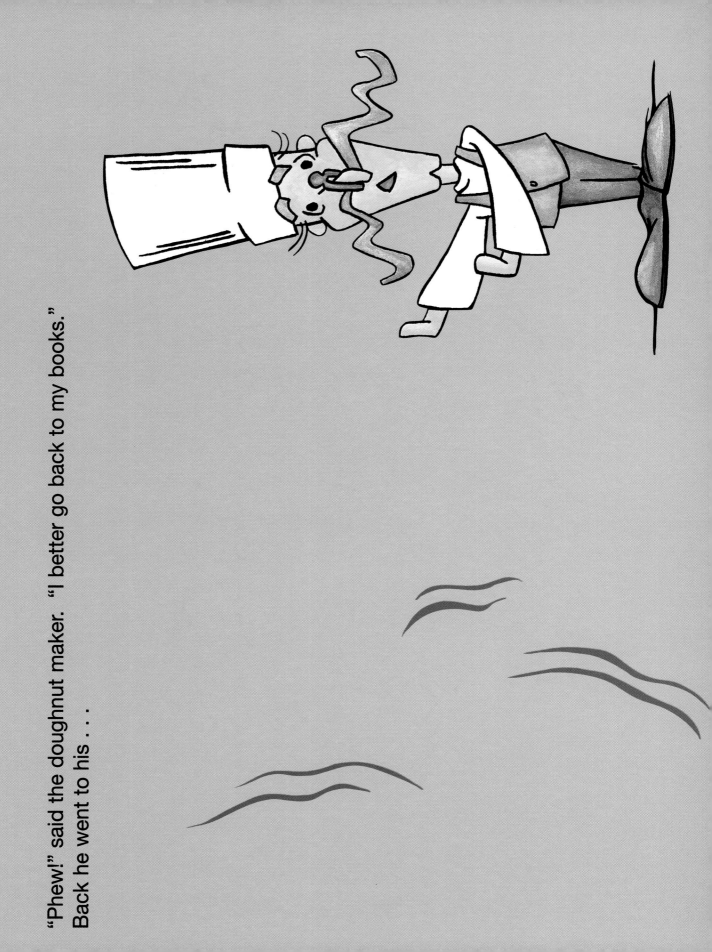

"Phew!" said the doughnut maker. "I better go back to my books."
Back he went to his . . . .

treasure maps,
ancient scrolls,
pop-up books
and tales of trolls.
He plotted stars,
telephoned Mars,
he hung from his toes
like a bat.
He buttoned a zipper,
tried on a flipper
and separated the split
from the splat.

Finally, the doughnut maker thought he was ready to work on the world again. He got out his bandsaw, his spackle, his salad tongs and, of course, the enormous mixing bowl, and added to the world . . . .

ladybug spots,
pink polka dots,
a saxophone player named Norm,
a poem by Poe,
a bean burrito,
a key, a kite and a storm.
He drilled.
He drained.
He stirred
and strained . . .

then microwaved the doughball on "high" for 4 hours (poking at it occasionally). However, the world he'd been working on all through the night— no matter from which angle you looked at it— still wasn't right.

The world was too lumpy (probably because of Norm).

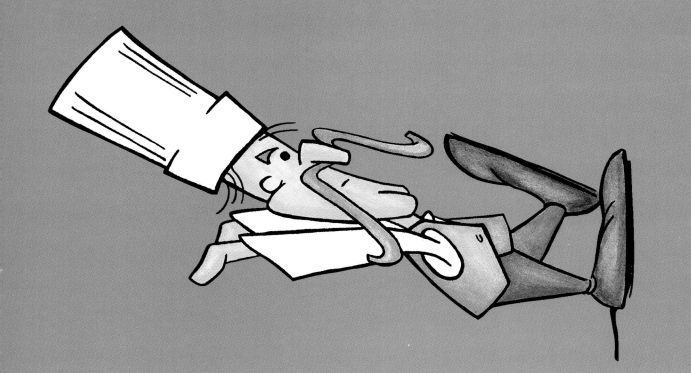

"Phooey," said the doughnut maker. He didn't give up though; he thought it would be pretty easy to correct the problem.

He looked left at right angles
and stood on his head,
looked up at the floor
and slept backwards in bed.
He rolled out the world,
and he balled it back up;
he added the rim
from a tiny teacup.
He flung the world 'round
and flattened it down.
He fried it in a skillet on "HOT."
He broiled it,
boiled it—
almost spoiled it—
and stewed it all night in a pot.

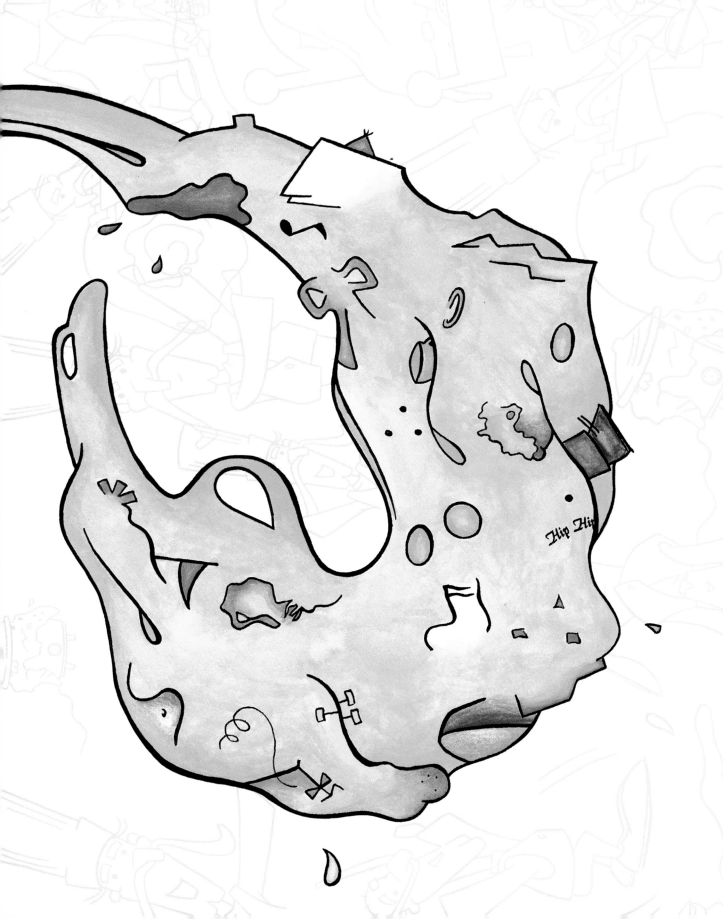

It was a good thing that the doughnut maker had anticipated beforehand that the making of a world would be an arduous task, because lately it was taking a great deal more effort to keep his wits about him. In the morning, he reluctantly noted that the world he'd been working on all through the night still, in the morning, wasn't quite right.

The world was too green.

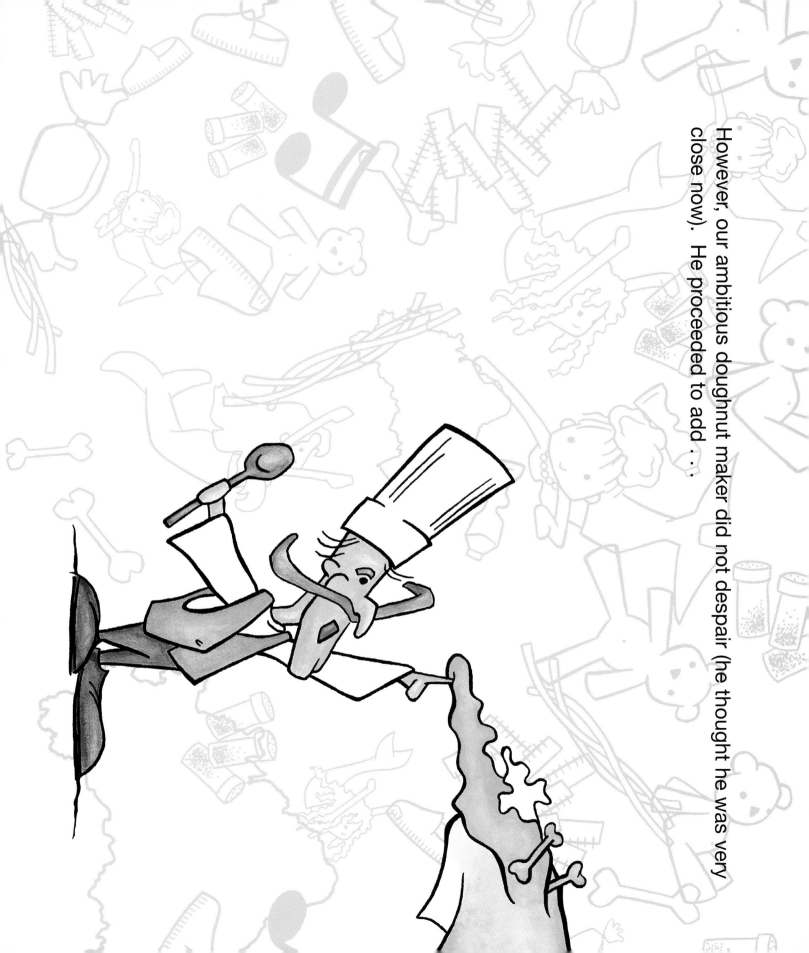

However, our ambitious doughnut maker did not despair (he thought he was very close now). He proceeded to add . . .

bubblegum toothpaste,
rhythm and blues,
mermaids,
teddybears
and 1,000 kazoos.
He tossed in ligaments
and rotten old bones,
salt-water taffy
and gallbladder stones,
then added galoshes
and a map of Brazil,
a pinch of ginger, jasmine and dill.

At this point, the doughnut maker decided to try a new approach: He hopped around his concoction doing the drizzle wizzle hoedown and chanting the first seven lines of "Mary Had a Little Lamb" in pig Latin. When he finished dancing, he was exasperated to discover that no matter which ear you held it up to . . .

the world was too noisy.

"Precisely!" shouted the doughnut maker as he slammed his dictionary shut with a thud. "A campfire is what this world needs!" That evening, with the help of scout troop 16, he roasted the world over a blazing fire and basted it with just the right amount of ghost story shivers, marshmallow goo, mosquito bites and hot-dog juice. However . . .

the world was too salty.

The doughnut maker was a bit shy of ambition at this point. His moustache drooped. His nose twitched. His eyes leaked. Even his hat collapsed. But he didn't despair for long; instead . . . .

he gathered his rolling pin, sugars and shakers
(all of the things familiar to bakers).
He sang his recipe
and whistled a tune.
He held fast to his bowl
and clung to his spoon.

Ingredients gyrated;
walls vibrated.
He snuck a taste of what he was making,
then added flour
and whistled louder;
he was so happy to find himself baking!
He waltzed 'round the room
and danced with a broom.
He held the mixture close to his heart.
The batter bounced.
The baker pounced.
He added laughter into his art.

Then, with a poke and a pat
and a simple "That's that,"
into the oven went his pastry delight.
With a hand to his head
he headed to bed
to dream about frosting all night.

But something rumbled.
The doughnut maker stumbled.
The oven started to shake.
Something caboomed
and va va vavoomed—
his kitchen started to quake.
In the light so luminous
hung a shape so voluminous!
The doughnut maker started to swoon.
People came running,
oohing and ahhing,
at the doughnut as big as the moon!

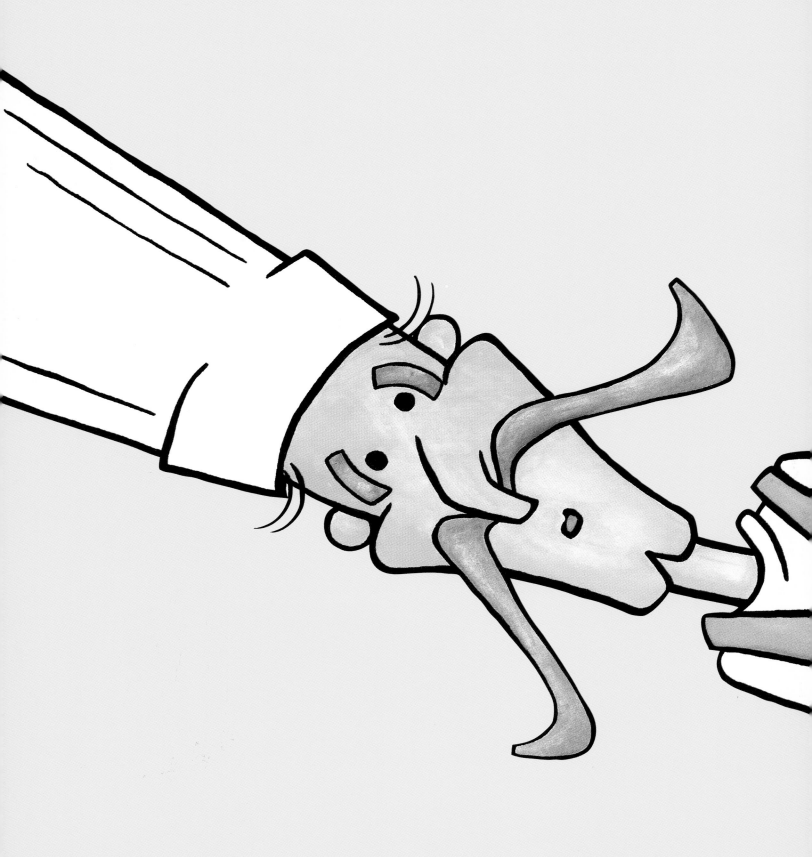

It was the grandest world that the doughnut maker had ever seen. It smelled like cinnamon (and nothing like sweatsocks). It looked dazzling, too, lobbed there with all of its charming lumps and bumps, browned to a beautiful bronze and basking in the glare from the sugary glaze. It hummed as it turned 'round in the warm kitchen, and when the doughnut maker tasted the bit left on his finger, he decided it was indeed the tastiest world he'd ever made (not even a pinch too much salt).

Yes, the world he'd been working on most of the night, (he was happy to note) finally was right.

And that is the end of the story.

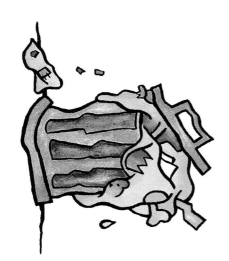